OKAY, WHAT-EVER.

I GUESS YOU DON'T MIND BEING MAULED BY MONKEYS.

HERE IS THE LAST GUY WHO READ THIS BOOK.

WAIT!!

DON'T TURN THE PAGE

To my favorite little monkeys, Aeryk and Grey – A. L.
For Hannah – M. F.

SIMON & SCHUSTER BOOKS FOR YOUNG READERS
An imprint of Simon & Schuster Children's Publishing Division
1230 Avenue of the Americas, New York, New York 10020
Text copyright © 2013 by Adam Lehrhaupt
Illustrations copyright © 2013 by Matthew Forsythe
All rights reserved, including the right of reproduction in whole or in part in any form.
SIMON & SCHUSTER BOOKS FOR YOUNG READERS is a trademark of Simon & Schuster, Inc.
For information about special discounts for bulk purchases, please contact Simon & Schuster Special Sales at
1-866-506-1949 or business@simonandschuster.com.
The Simon & Schuster Speakers Bureau can bring authors to your live event. For more information or to book an event, contact the Simon &
Schuster Speakers Bureau at 1-866-248-3049 or visit our website at www.simonspeakers.com.
Book design by Lucy Ruth Cummins
The text for this book is set in Matchwood WF.
The illustrations for this book are rendered digitally.
Manufactured in China
0613 SCP
Library of Congress Cataloging-in-Publication Data
Lehrhaupt, Adam.
Warning: do not open this book! / Adam Lehrhaupt ; illustrated by Matthew Forsythe.
p. cm.
"A Paula Wiseman Book."
Summary: Monkeys, toucans, and alligators unleash mayhem.
ISBN 978-1-4424-3582-7 (hardcover : alk. paper)
[1. Monkeys—Fiction. 2. Toucans—Fiction. 3. Alligators—Fiction. 4. Humorous stories.] I. Forsythe, Matthew, 1976– ill. II. Title.
PZ7.L532745 Do 2013
[E]—dc23
2012014432
2 4 6 8 10 9 7 5 3 1
ISBN 978-1-4424-3583-4 (eBook)

WARNING

DO NOT OPEN THIS BOOK!

NARRATED BY **ADAM** LEHRHAUPT

ILLUSTRATED BY MATTHEW FORSYTHE

A **PAULA WISEMAN** BOOK
SIMON & SCHUSTER BOOKS FOR YOUNG READERS
NEW YORK · LONDON · TORONTO · SYDNEY · NEW DELHI

Maybe you should put this book back.

You don't want to let the monkeys out.

Why did you turn the page?

Didn't you see the warning?

Stay on this page. You are safe here.

This is a good page.

I *like* this one.

Oh, no. Now you've done it.

What are they doing

What a mess!

Naughty mon keys.

It could be WORSE! Do not tempt fate by turning the page.

Please.

Monkeys *and*

toucans?

Can you stop now?
Everything used to
be so good.
Wait! Did you hear
that noise? That
didn't sound like . . .

monkeys. . . .

AN ALLIGATOR?!

This calls for extreme measures.
Only you can make things right.
You should set a trap!

This will surely work. It is a great trap.

ALLIGATORS **LOVE** TOUCANS AND MONKEYS.

TOUCANS AND MONKEYS <u>LOVE</u> BANANAS.

YOU CAN CATCH THEM <u>ALL</u> IN THIS BOOK!

THE PLAN

Quiet now. Don't scare them.

You need to be silent so they don't run away.

This is your big chance. . . .

When I say "go," you close the book.

Ready? Set!